Word Wise with Wordsworth

a wolf in sheep's clothing—someone who is secretly trying to do harm but seems friendly (**idiom, page 26**)

abandon—to leave empty (**verb, page 23,** *abandoned*)

alcove—a nook or small part of a room that is off to the side (**noun, page 22**)

available—easy to obtain or within reach (**adjective, page 8**)

beckon—to signal somebody to come closer (**verb, page 16,** *beckoned*)

bustle—to do something in an energetic way (**verb, page 12,** *bustled*)

clamber—to climb quickly or awkwardly (**verb, page 9,** *clambered*)

corridor—a hallway or passage between parts of a building (**noun, page 18**)

distracted—showing a lack of concentration (**adjective, page 10**)

employer—a person or business that hires and pays workers (**noun, page 14**)

extract—to pull something out, often using force (**verb, page 28,** *extracted*)

faint—not loud or clear (**adjective, page 27**)

impostor—someone who assumes a false identity (**noun, page 24**)

ordinary—usual or normal (**adjective, page 18**)

outstanding—excellent or terrific (**adjective, page 7**)

peculiar—odd or strange (**adjective, page 24**)

reputation—the way others view a person or thing (**noun, page 14**)

sputter—to make a popping or spitting sound (**verb, page 21,** *sputtered*)

stunned—shocked or amazed (**adjective, page 13**)

sturdy—made solidly (**adjective, page 16**)

superstitious—believing in luck, chance, or the supernatural (**adjective, page 11**)

TIME FLIES™ ♣ Book 8

A Wolf in Sheep's Clothing

by Quinn Alexander
Illustrated by Kelly Kennedy

SCHOLASTIC INC.

New York Toronto London Auckland Sydney
Mexico City New Delhi Hong Kong Buenos Aires

Abby was bubbling with excitement. For some time, she and Marco had been gathering information for a special project on the history of Cloverhill, the town where they lived. The day to start work on the actual report had finally arrived.

"So, what's the plan?" asked their teacher, Mrs. Harris. "Don't forget, you need a visual aid: something to show the class as you give your report."

"What about a big, huge poster?" Abby said. "Or maybe we could make our own history book, with pictures we draw. Or how about a newspaper—the *Cloverhill Times* from 100 years ago? That would be really cool."

"Those are **outstanding** ideas, Abby," Mrs. Harris said with a big smile.

But Abby wasn't done. "Wait! I have an even better one," she said. "What if we do something like the Cloverhill map?" she asked, giving Marco a meaningful look.

Marco knew right away what Abby was talking about: the strange map they had found in an old history book. Each time Wordsworth led them back in time, to the Cloverhill of 100 years ago, a building appeared on one of the map's streets—proof that they had really visited the past.

"Yeah, let's do *that*," he said slowly. "We can show what the houses and stores and stuff used to look like. But let's make it a three-dimensional map, like a little town for a model train set."

Abby's eyes sparkled. "Awesome! We'll need paint and glue and construction paper and small boxes to make the buildings."

"And a big piece of cardboard for the base," added Marco.

"Excellent!" said Mrs. Harris. "I'll go to the art room and see what supplies are **available**. In the meantime, remember what I always say: 'before you jump into a project . . .'"

"Think it through!" finished Marco and Abby.

"Think it through! Think it through!" Wordsworth repeated. But the moment Mrs. Harris was out of the room, he said something quite different, "Open the door! Open the door!"

Quickly Abby opened the cage door so that Wordsworth could start them on their adventure. Usually, he flew ahead to the magic doorway in Mr. Keys's room. This time, he just **clambered** onto Abby's shoulder, and she carried him there instead.

Mr. Keys was at his desk, doing paperwork. "Hello," he said. "Did you come for a visit?"

"Um . . . not exactly," said Abby.

"We need a big piece of cardboard for our history project," Marco said, thinking quickly. "Do you have one?"

"Check the supply shelves," said Mr. Keys. "You'll find what you're looking for there."

The kids hurried to the back of the room. The walls melted away, there was a loud pop and a flash of light, and they emerged in the past. They were standing by a cluster of maple trees in front of a large, two-story building.

"It's the Maplewood Inn," said Marco. "It looks almost the same as in our day."

"Didn't we meet one of the owners once, when we visited the past?" asked Abby.

"Yeah, Mrs. Russo," Marco replied. "Let's go inside and figure out why we're here."

Wordsworth flew up into a tree. "I'll stay outside," he said. "Mrs. Russo might be **distracted** by a feathered guest."

There was quite a hubbub in the lobby. A family of four was leaving the inn—and not in a happy mood. The father was talking loudly to a man with a large, droopy mustache. The man was clearly the manager of the place.

"I'm sorry, Señor Martinez, but we can't stay here any longer," said the father. "First there was sugar in the salt shaker and salt in the sugar bowl at dinner. Then we found muddy footprints leading nowhere in the bedroom. And last night, there were lights flashing on and off, and we heard moaning and groaning. It was terrible."

"And did you hear chains—how you say—clanking, too?" asked Señor Martinez.

"Yes!" the father exclaimed. "I'm not **superstitious**, but I would swear this place is haunted."

"Ah, the Maplewood ghost," Señor Martinez said sadly. "I, myself, do not believe in ghosts. But others, they feel differently; and they do not stay here long." He shrugged his shoulders. "You are sure you want to leave?"

"Absolutely," said the father, and his family nodded in agreement.

"Perhaps you should try the Crossroads Hotel," said Señor Martinez. "It's in Franklin, on Route 44 at the corner of Main Street. You can't miss it."

As the family left, Señor Martinez noticed Marco and Abby. He was about to say something, when Mrs. Russo **bustled** in. She recognized the kids immediately.

"Welcome to the Maplewood Inn. How nice to see you again," she said warmly. "Have you met Señor Martinez? We're so lucky to have him here. He's originally from Spain, and he's worked in the finest hotels in Europe."

Marco's family spoke Spanish at home. He thought Señor Martinez might like to hear his own language. "¡Hola! ¿Como estás?" he said, holding out his hand. "Me llamo Marco."

For a moment Señor Martinez looked **stunned**. Then he frowned. "Please! You must speak English," he said, ignoring Marco's hand. "It is not polite to speak in a language that others do not understand."

Marco blushed. "I'm sorry," he said to Mrs. Russo. "I just said, 'Hello. How are you? My name is Marco.' I didn't mean to be rude."

"Unlike *some* people," Abby said under her breath.

Señor Martinez turned his attention to his **employer**. "Señora Russo, more guests have left. They fear the ghost. I try to make them stay. I beg and plead. I say, 'There is no such thing as a ghost.' But they go anyway." He sighed deeply. "I have failed."

"Oh, dear," Mrs. Russo said. "We certainly can't afford to lose customers, but it isn't your fault. Old houses always creak and groan and make odd noises. People should understand that." She tried to smile. "Anyway, I came to tell you some good news: Senator Hoffman is arriving tomorrow, and he plans to stay several days. We'll need to get the best room ready for him."

"Do not worry. I will take care of everything," said Señor Martinez.

"Thank you," said Mrs. Russo. She turned to Marco and Abby. "Would you like a tour of the inn? My husband and I are proud of all the work we've had done. When we bought the place, it had been empty for a long time; and it was quite run-down. Maybe that's why it got a **reputation** for being haunted."

She showed the kids the sitting room and dining room. Then she led them through the kitchen, where staff members were preparing food, and out into the garden.

A gardener was weeding a muddy flower bed. "As you can see, this still needs work," Mrs. Russo said. "But doing it right costs money, and if we keep losing guests . . ."

Just then a dark-haired man appeared at the kitchen door. He **beckoned** Mrs. Russo.

"Oh, that's my husband. It looks as though he needs me for something," she said. "Enjoy the garden and take a peek at the rooms upstairs. Then come find me in the office."

She went inside, and Marco and Abby sat down on a **sturdy** wooden bench.

"OK, we know why we're here," said Abby. "It's to solve a mystery, right? Because I'm not buying the ghost story!"

"Me, either," said Marco. "I think someone's playing tricks on Mr. and Mrs. Russo."

"Or trying to wreck their business," said Abby. "We just have to figure out who it is."

"A cook or waiter could have switched the salt and sugar," Marco offered. "And a gardener could have left muddy footprints in a bedroom."

"But the footprints didn't go anywhere, which is weird," said Abby. "And what about the strange noises and flashing lights?"

Marco thought for a moment. "The fake ghost has to be someone who goes upstairs all the time, so it wouldn't be a big deal if anyone saw him."

"Let's check out the guest rooms," suggested Abby. "Maybe we'll find some clues."

They climbed a back staircase that led from the kitchen to the second floor. Then they wandered through the rooms. One was larger and fancier than the others—probably the room that the senator would stay in. But nothing seemed out of place or out of the **ordinary**.

"There's got to be a hidden passage that lets the fake ghost make noise and stuff without being seen," said Marco.

"*We* go through a secret door in the back of Mr. Keys's room," said Abby. "Maybe there's something like that here."

The two of them ducked into the closet at the far end of the fancy room. They tapped on the wood-covered walls. One wall sounded hollow! Marco pushed it gently, and it slid to the side. Before them was a dim **corridor**.

"Cool!" whispered Abby. "Let's see where it goes."

When they explored the narrow space, they discovered that the hidden passage ran in back of each guest room, and each closet had a sliding door.

They returned to the fancy room. "OK, we know how the fake ghost gets around," Abby said. "But who is he, and why is he haunting the inn?"

"I have a pretty good idea who he is," said Marco. "But we'll have to catch him to prove it."

"You're right." Abby agreed. "We need a plan—and we need to think it through."

The kids talked for a few minutes; then they got to work. Abby stuffed some spare pillows under the covers of the bed, to make the shape of someone sleeping. Marco closed the curtains so the room was dark. Then they slipped a Do Not Disturb sign over the doorknob and closed the door.

"What if we're wrong about the fake ghost?" Abby asked, as they went down the front staircase. "That could be pretty embarrassing."

"I'll give him a test," said Marco. "Then we'll know for sure."

The manager was at his desk in the lobby. "Ah, you are still here," Señor Martinez said. "What is it you want?"

"Um . . . we have a message for you," said Abby. "Senator Hoffman came a day early. He didn't want anyone to know about it, because he really, really needs to rest. He's already up in the best guest room, taking a nap."

"But . . . but . . . I have things I must prepare," Señor Martinez **sputtered**. Then he gave the kids a suspicious look. "This is not possible," he said. "I have been here all this time. No one has come to the inn."

"Mrs. Russo took him up the back staircase," said Abby. Then she lowered her voice. "I told you. It's a secret that he's here. No one is supposed to know."

"He's a very important man," Marco added. "Mrs. Russo wants his visit to be perfect."

Señor Martinez smiled. "I understand," he said. "I will see that he is not disturbed."

Marco smiled back. "Tú eres un mentiroso, cierto?" he said.

"Si, si. Of course," snapped Señor Martinez. "But I told you: do not speak Spanish."

"Sorry, I forgot," said Marco. He grabbed Abby's arm. "Come on. Let's go see if we can find a snack."

They set off toward the kitchen but ducked into an **alcove** in the sitting room instead. From their hiding place, they could see the front stairway.

"What did you say to Señor Martinez?" Abby whispered.

Marco grinned. "I said, 'You're a liar, right?' And he said, 'Yes, yes. Of course.' That was my test—and he flunked it."

"So he isn't really from Spain!" exclaimed Abby. "I *thought* his accent was fake. I bet his mustache is, too."

A moment later the manager **abandoned** his desk and hurried upstairs.

Marco and Abby raced to the office. "Mrs. Russo! Mr. Russo! Come quickly," said Abby. "We're about to trap your ghost."

Mr. Russo looked baffled. "Who are you? What do you know about the ghost?"

"We know someone's been playing tricks on your guests," said Marco. "If you come now, you can catch him in the act."

Mrs. Russo made a quick decision. "Let's at least take a look," she told her husband.

As they went up the back staircase, Marco told the Russos how he and Abby had set up the fancy room. Then they all tiptoed inside and took positions near the closet door.

Slowly the room filled with **peculiar** sounds—moaning and groaning, clinking and clanking. Then a beam of light flashed on and off, on and off.

Marco dashed to the secret panel and flung it aside. There was the fake ghost! He had a chain in one hand and a lantern in another. He blinked in surprise.

"Señor Martinez!" said Mr. Russo. He hauled the manager into the room.

Abby pulled back the curtains so everyone could see. "There's a secret passage behind all the rooms," she said. "He's been using it to scare away your guests."

"He's the fake ghost," said Marco. "And he's fake Spanish, too."

"Who are you, really?" demanded Mr. Russo.

The **impostor** stood up straight. "I'm Wendell Martin, and my family owns the Crossroads Hotel in Franklin."

"If your family owns a hotel, why did you come to work here?" asked Mrs. Russo.

"We lost business when you opened this inn," said Mr. Martin. "I had to put a stop to that—and scaring the guests away was easy. I used to come here as a kid, when the place was empty. That's when I found the secret passage." He sneered at the Russos. "It was right under your noses, and you never saw it."

"So all of your concern was just an act," said Mrs. Russo. "You're really **a wolf in sheep's clothing**!"

"I think it's time we had a talk with the police," said Mr. Russo.

He and his wife hustled Mr. Martin out of the room, forgetting all about Marco and Abby.

"Whew!" Abby said. "I would say we're done here."

Just then there was a new sound in the room—a **faint** *tap-tap-tap*. It was Wordsworth, tapping at the window. Marco let him in, and he flew to Abby's shoulder.

"Close the sliding door," said Wordsworth.

"That's a new one," said Marco. But he closed the sliding panel and waited to see what would happen.

"Open the door," said Wordsworth.

"This is crazy," said Marco. But he slid the door open.

Then Marco and Abby stepped into the dark corridor.

There was a pop and a flash of light, and they were back in
Mr. Keys's room.

"Did you find the cardboard?" Mr. Keys called.

The kids **extracted** a big piece from a supply shelf and carried
it to the front of the room.

"Thanks, Mr. Keys," said Abby. "We'll see you later."

They hurried back to the classroom and put Wordsworth in
his cage.

Then Marco checked the map. Just as he had hoped, the
Maplewood Inn had appeared.

Mrs. Harris returned with a load of art supplies, and the kids spread everything out on the worktable.

"Mrs. Harris? I have a question," said Marco. "Is there a hotel in Franklin called The Crossroads? It used to be at the corner of Route 44 and Main Street."

"There's nothing there now but a fast food place and some gas stations," Mrs. Harris replied. "So if it *was* there, it's long gone."

"Unlike the Maplewood Inn," said Abby.

"That's right," said Mrs. Harris. "That place will be around forever."

"Good work," said Wordsworth.

Get Your Word's Worth

After you finish reading this book together, use the prompts below to spark thoughtful conversation and lively interaction with your child.

♣ Some people who are **superstitious** have unique habits, such as stepping with their left foot first. What are some superstitions you believe in?

♣ A **sputter** is a popping or spitting sound. Name three things that make a sputtering sound.

♣ Show me how you would look if I just told you some news that made you look **stunned**.

♣ Do we have a **corridor** in our house? If so, let's **bustle** down it.